First Printing, 2023, Second Printing 2026

Note from the Author/Illustrator

This 2nd edition of Skud: A Visual Diary of Madness, has been re-worked from the ground up! All illustrations have been remastered, edited or replace entirely..Some of the illustrations were left relatively untouched while some are ccompletely new! The pages have been re-formatted and after years of learning, I am finally able to present "SKUD" in the way I have always intended! I hope you enjoy!

Love,
BUZZ

In loving memory of

Ray Woodrum

and

Larry Heller

A Visual Diary of Madness

Written and Illustrated
by Braxton Rosato

Chapter 1: Dinner of a Lonely Heart

"BZZZZZT...BZZZZT..."

"Huh?" says a man as his eyes open, bloodshot eyes, the kind you get after a long night of long drinking and snorting.

"What happened to you last night?" reads the text on his phone screen. The text was from Thorne, his best friend.

"Last night?" he whispers to himself.

Memories are sometimes hard to come by, even if it was in fact the night before, especially when you're trying to forget most nights.

Vague flashes of a slender man in his late twenties, wearing black jeans and a Hawaiian shirt, walking out of a bar bathroom.

He looks around, as he sees the pathetic walks of life mixed with what seem to be hot women, his gaze locks onto a set of immaculate breasts on a bombshell of a blonde.

We know this blonde must be at least forty but he's gonna ask her if she's 31 before he shoves his face in between her tits for a classic motorboat.

The next thing he remembers is him out back in

an alley somewhere, taking a long ass piss next to a dumpster.

"HEY MOTHERFUCKER!!" he hears from his left.

Two men's shadows start approaching, one a little more solid than himself and one small and fat.

Just as the men started to appear more man-like and less shadow-like, an aluminum bat was upside of his head! BAM! A right hook to the other side! BAM!

He was on his knees, cheek and nose bleeding profusely. The men laughed in front of him, proud of what they had done.

"Hey, cuck!!", he yelled out, "My turn…" and just like a lion would he pounced from off of the dank alley floor!

He started running at almost an inhuman speed. As he was running, he was prepping a monster right cross. When he arrived at his target, his punch met the taller man's face with the impact of a brick. Two teeth flew out of his cock-sucking mouth.

Before the man could even fall to the floor, he lifted him by the throat with his right hand into the air, against the wall and pulled his left hand back with an almost trance like focus. The man's eyes grew wide as he saw the hand enter his chest right where his heart was, before he could even let out a scream his heart was in the Hawaiian shirt man's hand...he dropped the limp body.

"WHAT THE FUCK?!!", screeched the portly man, "I gotta' get the hell outta' here!" The fat fuck turned tail like the little pig he was to run like he actually had a chance to escape.

"Where you goin' fat boy!" he said with a cigarette dangling in his mouth.

Now this is where we should know, this man in the Hawaiian shirt, was the star pitcher of his high school's baseball team back in Utah. That being said, the man set his feet, cocked his left hand back over his shoulder with the aforementioned ripped out heart, and let a fastball rip! SMACK!! direct hit, right to the back of the piggie's head. He came back to the edge of his bed to the sound of a feminine moan behind him.

"Where the hell did I get that cigarette from?" he said to himself and chuckled.

CHAPTER 2 : don't go breakin' my heart

"Thanks for bringin' me here last night," says a blonde woman from under the covers. "I don't know why my husband would leave me at that bar after you shoved your face in my tits."

It was in this moment that our gentleman here had realized who her husband was…one of the guys from the alley.

"Uh yeah, no problem…not to be a dick but you should probably leave. What was your name again?" said the black-haired man in a raspy voice, nothing a good tug of rum wouldn't fix.

Now this was a common theme in this guy's life, getting entirely too drunk and high on cocaine the night before and then waking up in bed with a random woman, at least it was at his place this time.

"Don't worry stud I gotta' get home anyway, my husband is probably freaking out." the blonde says as she pulls her dress over her voluptuous breasts and stands up. "Here's a little something for your scratches my husband and his friend gave you."

As she handed him what looked like 500 dollars, he thought,

"Wait? Did I even kill those guys?"

"Uh, thanks, I guess I'll see you around." He said as he was pulling on his jeans. The woman blew him a kiss and walked out of the door.

Just outside of the man's apartment the blonde woman started her walk of shame with a man watching her from his Edison across the street.

"There you are Mrs. Johnston" the man whispered to himself from behind his steering wheel as he drove off...

Meanwhile back in the man's apartment, he had walked into the bathroom to look at himself in the mirror. Some of the cuts and bruises had healed already but his eyebrow still had a cut.

"Ever since that camping trip when I was 17..."

His name is Skud.

He grew up in the Midwest, near the Utah border in a rather dysfunctional home, but a loving home. His father was a frequent binge drinker but always made time for him. His mother was a Native woman from a reservation that she had left when she was 14. In his early days Skud would play baseball, football, basketball and other sports, however he was especially talented at baseball, pitching to be exact.

When Skud was about 10 years old his mother died in a vicious car accident that some believed she purposefully caused to end her own life. After this young Skud was left with just his father, who completely descended into heavy drinking after the "accident." This left Skud to fend for himself most of the time, but his father always encouraged his baseball aspirations, lead parents and umpires quite frequently at his games.

Shortly after his 15th birthday his dad went off the deep end, all pun intended, and jumped off a bridge drunk as shit, dying on impact with the water. Skud was truly alone now...crashing on various friends and obscure relatives' couches for the next few years.

During one of these couch surfing sessions, he was offered an opportunity to go camping with his friends and his friend's dad who was an avid camper...

CHAPTER 3 : HEART OF THE WILD

For the camping trip, it was Skud, 3 of his buddies and one of their dads, Ron. Now Ron was real deal camper and planned for them to be out in the wilderness for 4 days. Pretty standard camping shit, drinking beers and chopping wood, however, Ron was an avid arrowhead hunter as well. So, around the fire on the first night, he told stories of how the native people to the land had been very spiritual and possessed very "out there" beliefs.

One such story that stuck out for Skud, being half native himself, was the belief that when you killed an animal or warrior in battle some tribes would eat their kill's heart to gain their strength. Such a wild belief couldn't be true. Could it?

On the second day they all went on an arrowhead digging trip a few paces from their campsite. Skud had managed to find an arrowhead made of obsidian on his dig and kept it as a souvenir. Later that night they were around the campfire drinking beers and just having a good time. Skud had brought some pot with him to smoke because it helped him sleep and hell, he just enjoyed being high. After a few beers Skud had to take an unusually long piss as per usual. So, he got up from around the fire and went to his tent to grab his bowl and sack of weed and then said to the others, "Hey, I'm going to take a leak!"

As Skud walked through the trees surrounding their campsite he looked up and saw how bright and full the moon was that night, so he decided this was as good a place as any to smoke a bowl. He sat on a rock, loaded his bowl and started smoking after he took a leak on some trees. He gazed out at the moon which was right over the tree line across a small valley and thought of his parents, and how much his friends meant to him. Just as he was about to walk back to the campsite, he saw a wolf standing in the field in front of the trees, staring at him, eyes golden with the moon glistening off them. Skud stared back.

The wolf took one step, another step, another step and then started running full speed at Skud! Before he could even react, the wolf was sinking its teeth into his left arm tearing at his flesh, he fell to the ground.

The wolf was mauling Skud's left arm, searing pain shooting up his entire arm. He thought, "This is it, I'm gonna' fucking die out here."

Just then he felt something digging into his side from his right pocket…the arrowhead! He reached in his pocket with his right hand as fast as he could while struggling with the wolf on his other arm…

he grabbed the arrowhead and in one swift motion stuck it in the wolf's eye! The wolf jumped off of Skud and whimpered. He pressed his counterattack and grabbed the wolf with his mangled arm around its neck and pulled the arrowhead out of the wolf's eye then used it to slit its throat.

The wolf was dead and Skud's arm was bleeding bad, not to mention all the other scratches and gashes he had gotten wrestling the bastard. He knew that they were miles from the nearest hospital and in his adrenaline/pot fueled thought process he remembered the stories about eating your enemy's heart, in this moment he made a decision he could never take back…he decided to eat the wolf's heart to save his arm and gain its strength. He used the arrowhead to cut the wolf's chest open, the pain was starting to become unbearable, he cut aside the flesh and felt around the cavity until he felt the heart…he ripped as hard as he could, and the heart came out. The warm blood was flowing down his hand, he looked up at the moon and took a bite out of the heart. Warm blood filled his mouth and he wanted to gag but he knew he needed to swallow if this insane idea was even remotely going to work, oh well too late.

Skud fell to his knees and choked as he started dry heaving, his whole body felt like it was on fire, something weird was happening, his vision was blurring, his breathing getting heavier and then he rolled to his back looking up to the moon as his eyes closed…darkness……screams……crying……blood……death….

CHAPTER 4: SHOT TO THE HEART

When Skud finally came to it was almost dawn. He looked around, vision still blurry, and saw he was standing at his campsite. As he looked around his vision slowly started to clear, and he could see that all the tents were ripped to shreds and covered in blood. In a frenzy Skud ran to the first tent he saw on the right to check on his friends only to see the mangled body of his first friend inside, Skud immediately started to vomit profusely.

After composing himself as much as he could, Skud dared to check the second tent and then third tent only to find the same grisly scene.

"HELLLLLLPPPP!!!!" Skud screamed as loud as he could as he fell to the ground and started to whimper.

Confused, angry and exhausted he just laid there on the dew-covered morning ground with no reply to his call for help and in that moment, he knew he was truly alone. Sometime later the sun had come up and brought even more horror to Skud's nightmare, if only he could wake up. As he rose from the ground, he looked at his hands and saw that his arm that the wolf had mauled was completely healed as well as his other cuts and bruises.

"Oh wow, it worked." He said to himself softly, still no one around to hear his cry for help, "That's pretty—" as he looked at his hands closer, he saw that he had claw like fingernails and a lot more blood on his hands than he had when he fainted.

"No, it can't be!?" he said in horror as he tasted more blood in his mouth. Skud wasn't a fool he already knew what he had done, somehow after he had passed out, he wandered back to the camp and viciously murdered his friends and one of their dads in their sleep…somehow. But how? So many questions and so many different emotions to process, he just couldn't understand it, so he sat there for a while, just sat there……

Once reality had set in for Skud, at what appeared to be 3PM he knew he had to leave, he knew he had to go and never come back. So, in that moment he came up with an easy plan, he would fake his own death or at the very least be considered dead in the woods. He got up off the ground threw off his dirty and blood-stained clothes, put on the clean set he had in his camping bag and just left. He walked and walked and walked some more until he was exhausted, which took a lot longer than usual, almost like he had in fact absorbed that wolf's strength somehow. He decided to go climb a tree to sleep in he saw nearby and just passed out.

When Skud awoke he was in a state of panic, he fell from the tree onto the cold morning ground. COUGH COUGH it felt like his rib was cracked as he coughed and blew out dirt and grass from his mouth. He quickly sprung up and looked at his hands…they were normal and didn't have any blood on them, just dirt from his trek.

"Oh, thank God" he said as he let out a sigh of relief, confident he hadn't murdered anyone in his sleep again. Skud got up off the ground and just started walking again until he found a creek nearby to splash water on his face. After he was done splashing water on his face and taking some swigs from the creek, he kept walking…and walking. When nightfall arrived Skud started to notice a glow above the trees…city lights. Full of excitement, he started running full speed in the direction of the lights, legs intensely burning, he made it to the edge of the trees. He walked out of the trees and right in front of him only a few miles away he saw it…Pepper Mountain City.

CHAPTER 5: HEART OF GLASS

Skud took a swig from his rum bottle as he looked in the mirror, it helped him to cope. After looking at the money he had been given on the end table he said,

"Well, I guess it's time to go see Sal."

Sal was Skud's bookie and seeing how much he liked to gamble, also his long-time friend. He put on a t-shirt, threw on his hoodie and walked out the door. As he was walking down the corridor, he could smell the mix of everyone's cooking in the apartment building—that, and piss along with the complete degradation of society, nice neighborhood…

He came out of the building onto the sidewalk, the street was bustling with cars and people seeing as it was 2 in the afternoon. Good morning. Skud started to walk down the street towards Sal's place a few blocks away so he could put in a bet for the game tonight, the New York Goals were in town to play Skud's favorite team, the Utah Opera. As he was walking down the street he saw two men with identical haircuts, both wearing black pants, a white dress shirt and a black tie. "Excuse me sir do you have a minute to—", before they could finish their sentence Skud interrupted, "I'm running late for work, no time."

"Fuckin Former Day Saints." he muttered to himself as he walked away briskly, dragging at his cigarette. He didn't in fact have a job, he was going to see his bookie, Sal.

The Former Day Saints are a religious group that "originally" colonized Utah and still wield massive legislative power there, particularly in Pepper-Mountain City, Skud's "home." They send people out to convert a dying city, infested with crime while they drive around in fancy self-driving Edison's, Skud didn't have time for that shit today he needed to gamble and drink.

Ever since the camping incident, Skud had been living in Pepper-Mountain City, mostly working debt-collecting jobs for the local crime family and their bookies, that's how he met Sal. Sal was your typical grease ball bookie, about 60 years old, jaded by a life of crime, wearing the wife beater shirt and all, but he had a soft spot for Skud. A few years back Skud had been on a bender as per usual and started feeling sentimental, so he stumbled over to Sal's to tell him how good of a friend he had been to him. When he got to the front door, he knocked, only to find that the door had already been kicked open. In a drunken moment of clarity, he slowly crept into Sal's living room, so he wouldn't be heard, only to see him tied to a chair being beaten and questioned by a large Former Day Saint. Long story short, Skud bashed the

FDS over the head with the bottle he had been swigging, untied Sal and threw the FDS down the apartment steps. Him and Sal have been close ever since.

"Hey, you son of bitch!" Sal said in a friendly tone to Skud, getting up from his recliner, as Skud walked through his door, "How was your night killer?"

"Don't ask." Skud replied as he shook Sal's hand and gave him a hug.

"Who you got tonight brother?" said Sal, "Let me guess, The Opera?"

"You fuckin know it" Skud said as he pulled a beer from Sal's fridge.

"You know, there's more to life than gambling, drinkin' and fuckin' Skud. Maybe you should settle down with one of those broads you always talk about." Sal said as he pulled his folder out with his betting info.

Skud walked over to Sal's fish tank and tapped on the glass. "Hey fishy fishy" he said in the tone one would use with a toddler.

"Alright, The Opera are a 9-point underdog, how much you want?" Sal shouted from across the room.

"Give me 250 on the Opera to win by 10." Skud replied. He sat down and waited for Sal to finish whatever it was he did, downing the rest of his beer.

"Here ya go, 250 on the Opera. Where ya headed bud?" Sal said as he handed Skud his betting slip.

"Titty bar, you comin?" replied Skud.

"It's 2 in the afternoon for Christ's sake I got shit to do, but I'll meet you there later.... Be careful kiddo." Sal said to Skud as he walked him to the door and patted him on the back.

"You too" said Skud as he walked out of Sal's door, back onto the streets towards his favorite bar, Puss N' Boots.

The strip club was only a few more blocks past Sal's place, enough of a distance for Skud to see the filth he was surrounded by. Even though the city was run by a religious group, it was rife with crime and degeneracy, nude bars on every corner, liquor stores on every street and the homeless everywhere you look. Along his way Skud walked by droves of homeless people sleeping on the streets, most of which asked him for money not realizing he was just as poor as them, just luckier and better looking. The same reply to everyone who asked,

"I would if I could man", technically he could, seeing as he had 250 left from the 500 after his bet, but that was just begging to be spent…at the strip club.

So, Puss N' Boots wasn't exactly the best titty bar in town, but they had fairly few rules and strong drinks, Skud's favorite. When he was rounding the corner and could see the sign of the club at the end of the street, he lit up a cigarette, turning around with his hand cupped to avoid the wind, he noticed an Edison that appeared to stop when he turned around.

"Huh, that's odd." He said as he turned back around walking towards the strip club, puffing his bogey.

When he got to the door, he saw one of his favorite things, a flashing neon OPEN sign that said 24 hours. "I'm home" Skud thought as he walked through the door into the dark hallway leading into the showroom. As he walked down the hallway he saw his favorite bouncer, Cliff, who shook his hand and waved him through the curtain to the floor. When Skud peeled through the curtains, he was hit with an aroma of mixed perfumes, fog machine and flashing lights, his paradise.

He walked over to the bar where the bartender Jimmy, a 50 something ex wise guy, already had a rum and coke poured for Skud. In 10 seconds, the drink was gone,

"Another one Jimmy." said Skud. Jimmy poured the drink and Skud walked to "his" table in the middle of the floor, in front of the stage and sat down, taking a swig of his drink...

231
233
235

CHAPTER 6: HEARTBREAKER

There are very few things better in this world than a naked woman dancing in front of you. She might not have been Skud's favorite girl, but she would do for now. He got up out of his chair, went over to the bar and exchanged a 100-dollar bill for one -hundred one-dollar bills. As soon as the chick dancing saw Skud walking over with his wad of cash, she directed her attention to him.

"How you doin' tonight baby?" She said while rubbing her bare tits and leaning backwards on her knees, she knew him very well since he was in 3 nights a week, these girls were like his family…. that he fucks.

"I'm doing alright, how's your pussy smell tonight?" Skud replied.

"Fuck you Skud." She said as she clapped her 8-inch heels together.

After throwing 7 ones on the stage, the stripper leaned in and kissed Skud on the cheek while handing him a bag of white powder which was cocaine.

"Thanks." he said and walked back to the bar to grab another drink. (Skud repeated this routine for about 4 hours with frequent trips to the bathroom to snort coke.)

DRIN

With what had to be his fifteenth drink in hand, he was headed to the bathroom to do another fat line of blow. Skud pulled the bag out of his pocket and dumped a hefty amount of powder on the screen of his phone, on the back of the toilet, chopped it down to a powder using a bill and a lighter.

"SSSNNNNNFFFFTTT.... oh yeahhhh, I'm back baby!!" he said out loud after blasting a hog leg. While licking the cocaine residue off of his phone screen he saw that Thorne had texted him again.

Cleaning off his nose and walking out of the bathroom, he noticed two men in all black suits. One man was a little taller than Skud but in way better shape, the other one, a mountain of a man and bald. They looked like some of Gino Tallarico's henchman, the leader of the family that Sal was affiliated with.

Give me tiiiimmme...to reaaalize my criiiimes...

"My favorite Culture Club song" Skud said to himself walking towards the gentlemen, hand slightly raised. Wouldn't you know it right as Skud was about to signal them towards him he saw the slender one of the two reach into his blazer pocket, pull out a handgun and shoot Cliff in the face at point blank range. He knew these guys weren't here to talk.

The gunshot sent the strip club into a panic, naked strippers in heels started running for cover and then the slender man handed the handgun to the larger man while he pulled out an Uzi from the other side of his blazer. BBBBBLLLLLLL-LLLL-LAAAATTTTT!!!! Automatic gunfire erupted from the slender man's hand in Skud's direction, mirrors and glasses shattered everywhere as he started running towards the bar for cover, narrowly avoiding being shot. BOOM! Jimmy the bartender had grabbed a double-barreled shotgun from under the bar and fired it at the men, he missed.... the Uzi didn't. Skud leapt over the bar with bullets flying past him and slid over to where Jimmy was choking on his own blood, shotgun on the ground.

"I'm sorry Jimmy" Skud said as he picked up the shotgun from the ground.

"You still alive you fuckin' prick??!!" shouted the slender man as he dropped the magazine out of his gun onto the floor and started digging into his pocket for a reload. Leaning against the bar, Skud thought to himself,

"This is it man, it's do or die. Right now." He took a deep breath, exhaled and popped up from behind the bar, shotgun ready to fire and...BOOM!! Direct hit to the center of the slender man's chest, he fell to the floor. Two bullets from the Cue Ball's pistol went over Skud's head as he ducked back under the bar. He could hear the clicks from the Cue Balls gun as he tried to keep firing…empty. Skud opened the shotgun, popped out the two spent shells and started frantically looking for bullets but before he could even see where they were he heard a thud and felt two massive hands on his shoulders.

"Shitttttt!" he said as he was lifted from the floor behind the bar, dropping the shotgun.

The larger man (Cue Ball) had yanked Skud up from behind the bar and put him on the bar top, he wrapped his ham hocks around Skud's throat and started squeezing. With his oxygen in short supply, Skud started punching the bald bastard with his left hand to no avail while trying to feel for the shotgun he knew he dropped nearby… he couldn't find it…this was it, dying in a titty bar, I suppose there's worse ways to go. Skud's vision started to go dark, his body went limp and right as he was about to check out, the pressure around his throat let up…one of the strippers had taken off one of her dancin' shoes and hit cue ball in the head!! He only had a split second as the cue ball slapped the stripper to the ground with massive force, but that's all Skud needed. He grabbed the shotgun from the floor and hit Cue Ball in the face with the butt of the shotgun as he turned around. As the large henchman was stumbling backwards from the hit, Skud flipped the shotgun in the air and caught it by the barrel. He gripped it like a baseball bat, cranked it back.

"Batter up" Skud said as he ripped a line drive straight to right titty off Cue Ball's head, he fell to the floor twitching.

Skud wasn't finished, he looked around and saw at least three strippers on the ground either dead or hurt. He snapped. He looked at Cue Ball twitching on the ground with blood leaking from his mouth and head,

"Let's bring these runners home" Skud said as he lifted the shotgun butt over what was left of Cue Ball's head and started smashing into it until there was nothing but skull fragments and brain matter where a head used to be.... Game over.

CHAPTER 7 : CLOSER TO THE HEART

"What'a, we got?" said detective Moe Scheffield as he flicked his cigarette, exhaled, walked under the yellow Caution tape and into Puss N' Boots. Moe Scheffield was a tall, slender man with flowing blonde hair, a decorated officer with a slightly violent record. He got to detective the old-fashioned way, with his fists…

"It ain't pretty Moe" replied the street cop as he pulled back a plastic curtain onto the dance floor.

It was a grisly sight to behold, blood and shattered glass strewn all about and not to mention, dead people. Moe did a body count,

"One, two, three, four…four dead strippers, a dead bartender and two mob guys." he said, strapping on a rubber glove and pulling a cigarette from his soft pack with his mouth and lighting it.

Moe walked past Cue Ball's headless body and gagged a little bit to himself from the sight. He took some steps across the bar and past the dance floor while stepping over two dead strippers on his way to the slender mafioso lying on his back with a hole in his chest. Moe squatted near the man's left shoulder and started looking him up and down, eventually focusing his attention on the chest wound. He pulled the man's black lapel to the side with his gloved hand while taking a drag from his cigarette with his other hand, exhal-

ing emphatically.
When the tag became exposed, Moe's eyebrows raised.
"Made with the guidance of the Lord by the FDS" said the detective to himself out loud. "Hey officer! Whaddya make of this?" he shouted to the cop who let him onto the scene who was only a few feet away.

The officer walked close to the corpse and saw Moe pointing to the tag inside the man's jacket,

"If these are mob guys, what are they doing in FDS made clothes? I thought those guys hated each other?" said the young officer.

"My thoughts exactly.... Gomez, was it?" replied Moe "and look at that wound" he continued.
"Shotgun blast to the chest? We found one by the bar" said Gomez curiously.

"Yeah, it appears so, but...there's another wound in this bastard's chest" said Moe as he peeled off his rubber glove.

forty-seven minutes earlier

Skud tossed the shotgun back over towards the bar after completing his grand slam on Cue Ball's head and looked around the strip club at the devastation. He looked a few feet away and saw

Spyder, his favorite girl lying face down with one heel on, she was the one who had saved Skud's life. Skud rushed to where she was laying and flipped her over. Spyder was a beautiful, naturally brunette girl in her early 20's and covered in tattoos, but she was wearing a blonde wig tonight. He called out her name, "Spyder!" as he patted her cheek a few times and felt her pulse.... nothing......the blow from Cue Ball had killed her...

Cughhh..glurrghhh.... Skud looked up while holding Spyder's lifeless body, a single tear rolling down his cheek and saw where the sound had come from...the slender man was still alive and gasping for air across the bar.

"Motherfucker" Skud said while standing up, wiping away his lone tear. He walked across the club, through overturned tables and carnage to where the man was lying on his back. When Skud got to the man he leaned down and grabbed the man with both of his hands by the man's collar and shouted while lifting him slightly,

"Who sent you, you son of a bitch??!!!"

The man smiled with blood in his teeth and coughed at Skud,

"Cough...Cough...you...agghh...."

Skud shouted, "What the fuck do you mean shit head??!!!" The slender man's eyes began to close and Skud shook him some more…

"Cough…agghhh…. last niiggh…cough…agghhh…Fuck you!" said the man as he spit some blood in Skud's face. Skud winced, wiped the blood-spit from his face and reached his right hand back while holding the man's lapel and thrust his hand into the man's open shotgun wound and ripped his heart clean out…. while pulling back his hand Skud noticed the tag on the inside of the man's lapel….

made with the guidance of the lord, by the FDS….

"Shiiiittt" said Skud as he dropped the man's limp body, tossed the heart, and made for the back door, through the dressing room.

Skud made his way into the dressing room and looked around inside for any signs of life…. nothing…just your typical messy strip club dressing room. He started walking towards the back exit at the end of the dressing room when he heard a whimper, a soft whimper... Skud looked over by one of the lockers to the right of where he was and saw a little girl curled up on the floor of the locker. The little girl looked up at Skud, her eyes filled with tears and longing, he recognized the eyes from…somewhere……Skud knew the right thing to do was to look after her since her mother was probably dead, but he just kept walking… right out the back door

"Next time kid…" he said to himself while walking out the door… "next time…"

Back at the crime scene

"Detective!! We got someone back here!!" shouted Gomez as he carried the little girl from the dressing room to the main area of the club. While Gomez was still holding the little girl in his arms, detective Moe Scheffield asked her, "Where is your mommy?" Squealing and leaning her face into Gomez' shoulder, the little girl pointed to Spyder's dead body… "My god…" said Gomez as he put his closed fist to his mouth. "My God too…" replied Moe as he took a long drag from his cigarette…...

"My God too" …...

Chapter 8: heartbreak hotel

Skud ran out the back door of Puss N' Boots and into the dank alley behind it. He only had two choices, left or right, he went left. Skud started running lightly as to not draw any attention to himself in the alley, which was its own ecosystem in and of itself. The Alleys of pepper-mountain city were riddled with trash and bums, real fucking FILTH. The back side of this city was even more depraved and disgusting than the front side. Skud kept his pace past a group of bums around a trash can fire fighting over what looked like the rotten leg of a dog on the right. Skud saw several similar groups doing this same practice and some having sex with each other along his way through 5 blocks of alley…a real scenic route, and sadly nothing out of the ordinary for this God-forsaken city.

Skud finally got far enough through the hell that was the alleys of pepper-mountain city to where he felt he could pop back out onto the streets, and he did. When he stepped back out onto the sidewalk from the alley he reached into his pocket and pulled his phone out. He looked at the screen and he saw that there was blood all over his hand from when he ripped that prick's heart out, whatever. One ring…two rings…

"Yoo!" Thorne said from the other line of the phone, "What's up?"

"Ain't shit man, you at home?" replied Skud.

"Of course bro, I haven't been to sleep yet." Thorne said as Skud turned a corner with both hands in his pockets, holding his phone between his shoulder and neck, nodding his head at people walking past him.

"Alright, I'm on the way over." Skud said and then hung up the phone, picking up his pace.

Skud kept walking down the streets towards where Thorne lived, his hood up, covering his head. He was headed to Thorne's place, Vehr Drive. Yes, Vehr Drive, a place that Skud hung out with regularly. Thorne was a guy that Skud hung out with regularly, drinking, snorting, gambling and whoring, essentially, he was his best friend. They had met 5 years back through some mutual friends. It was only a few blocks from where Skud was and thank God for that, guess it was time for Skud to put on his "happy face" as in, to appear like he didn't just kill two people viciously. Simple enough. After walking a 3 more blocks the sun started to fade and night was setting in and there Skud stood waiting for the light to change so he could cross over into the south side of town, right onto Thorne's Street.

Thorne lived about 3 blocks into Vehr Drive, a name affectionately given to a particularly darker part of pepper mountain city, the part of town only acceptable for a certain type of degenerate… Thorne was one of those people. Despite the bad rap, the street was quite the haven for people like Skud and Thorne, guys who lived outside of the law, usually under fake names or aliases, scheming all along the way. Thorne was located in an apartment building inside of the Oakbrook Projects, a low-income apartment complex made up of 2 four-plex style apartments divided by a parking lot down the middle…paradise.

Skud could hear music and female laughter coming from Thorne's open window as he walked towards the parking lot. He walked across the lot, into the building and up the steps to the door. Before he could even knock, the door flung open and there stood Thorne shirtless, arms open waiting for a hug.

"Come here you son of a bitch" Thorne said as he pulled Skud in for a hug, patting him on the back. "We got booze and girls, booze and girls…I don't know, do you?" he said, and they both started laughing.

"Ahhh, good to see you man" replied Skud, "You got a fuckin beer?" he continued.

"Of course I do, the girls just made a run, gonna' pregame before we hit the town apparently" replied Thorne, wiping his nose as he inhaled hard.

As Skud walked into the apartment, following Thorne he could hear two female voices talking and giggling.

"I'm gonna' take a piss quick" Skud said, keeping his bloodied hand concealed in his pocket as he turned right into Thorne's bathroom.

"Alright you want a line?" Thorne shouted to Skud through the now closed bathroom door. "Hell yeah man" said Skud, turning on the faucet and looking into the smudged mirror. He put his hands under the water and started rubbing until the dried blood started rinsing off into the sink and down the drain. Looking into the mirror he whispered to himself, "Alright bro, game face." Shaking his hands into the sink and drying his hands on his pants he went to open the bathroom door.

When Skud walked through the hallway from the bathroom into the living room he was greeted by the sight of Thorne chopping up several lines of cocaine on his coffee table flanked by two wom-en, Layla and Tabitha. Layla and Tabitha were for lack of a better term Skud and Thorne's "Fuck Buddies" or "Coke Whores" depending on who you ask.

"Skud, where have you been? We've been partying since you left the bar!" shouted Tabitha as she motioned Skud to sit next to her, which he did. Tabitha was the one of the two that Skud fucked regularly, beyond that they actually had a lot in common, they both liked cocaine, art and psychedelics but most importantly, Theory, Skud's favorite band. Chicks like Tabby were rare to find in today's age and hell it would be a lie to say Skud hadn't told her he loved her a bunch of times, so he kept her around. Now Layla, oh Layla. She was the love of Thorne's life for some God-awful reason even though she was openly the village bicycle and rarely reciprocated love to him, but nevertheless a pretty cool chick to party with.

Putting his arm around Tabitha on the couch Skud said, "Well I remember going to the bar with you guys and drinking but then it all got a little fuzzy. I woke up and came here."

"Well, you piece of shit," Tabitha said as she snorted up a line of coke off of the table, "you really had us worried."

"Oh, I'm sure you were just distraught." Skud said laughingly as he rolled up a left-over bill from the strip club and went in for a toot. "SSSNNNNFFFFTTT… ohhh yeeahhh… that'll do pig!"

1:18
UNKNOWN CALLER
INSMING CALL

CHAPTER 9: THE TAHOE

After about an hour and a half of excessive drinking and several lines of cocaine, it was time to hit the town.... again. Skud, Thorne and the girls stumbled boisterously out of Thorne's apartment, beers in hand down the steps and into Thorne's car, The Tahoe. The Tahoe was a large white SUV with years of partying engraved into the seats, a real battlewagon, Skud couldn't count the times it had gotten him home safely. Once they were all loaded in, Thorne at the helm and Skud riding shotgun, they were off into the night.

Despite it's rather rocky start the night was shaping up to be a good one, the girls were in the backseat drinking away, Thorne was singing along to the songs on the radio and Skud felt content (a rare feeling for sure). As they made their way out of Vehr Drive and into the city Thorne suggested going to Puss N' Boots, an idea Skud quickly but casually shot down, so they decided on Feathered Indians, a Hip-Hop/Country Fusion club. The drive was going pretty standard as far as a trip in The Tahoe could go when Skud noticed something funny in the side-view mirror, an Edison following closely behind them. They made a few more turns in the direction of the bar, the Edison following every move until they stopped at a stop light.

"Huh a little late for Former Day Saints." Skud said out loud and before anyone in the vehicle could reply another Edison screeched out in front of them.

Two men in matching suits rushed out of the car towards them, guns drawn and before Skud could shout out for Thorne to accelerate, a hand with a gun reached in the passenger window and smashed him right in the face…darkness.

When Skud came to, everything was still dark, and he could feel the sticky blood on his face sticking to whatever was covering his head. Confused, he shouted out through his face covering and tried to move, he couldn't, he could feel that he was tied to a chair, just then he heard a door open and footsteps coming in his direction.

"Hey you motherfucker! What is this shit?!" Skud shouted as the covering was removed from his head and he saw two white men in matching suits who looked identical to one another, both with dark hair and dark eyes. SLAP!! The man on the left immediately struck Skud without saying a word. CCCRRRAAAACCKKK! Now the man on the right. The man on the left cocked his hand back for another blow but then the man on the right raised his hand as if to halt his action and he spoke,

"Now tell me, Skud is it? Why are you involving yourselves with the Lord's affairs?"

"What?" Skud replied. The man looked at the other man and nodded. WWHHAAPP!! A heavy right hook.

"I'll ask you again, WHY ARE YOU INTERFERING WITH THE WILL OF GOD!!"

This time the man didn't wait for a reply he just hit Skud hard as fuck again. Just as the two men were cocking their hands back for a slug fest the door swung open again and they immediately stiffened up at the sight of the man who walked through the door.

The man was in an immaculate suit, red embroidered vest underneath a pristine white jacket with matching white pants. His hair was radiant blonde, slicked back perfectly, his eyes a piercing blue, a tall and fit man a little over six feet tall. Silence was over the room, which Skud could see was an interrogation room of some sort as the man walked over to the two standing men.

"Well now this simply won't do" the man in white said, "This man is our guest. Is this how we treat our guests?? Untie him immediately."

The two men immediately jumped at the order and untied Skud.

"I'm so sorry my son" the man in white continued,

"This has been an egregious mistake. Let's go have a chat."

Skud stood up from the chair rubbing his wrists and looking at the two men in matching suits he said, "I'll catch you boys on the flip-side."

The man in white pulled out a red silk handkerchief from his lapel and handed it to Skud. "Here, clean yourself up a bit my friend" he said as he motioned Skud out of the room and into a hallway.

Skud took the handkerchief as they walked, wiped his face a bit with it and handed it back, "So uh thanks for the help and all but uh what the fuck is going on?" said Skud as he walked with the man into a cement hallway and down the corridor past several doors until they reached an elevator.

"Patience my friend" said the man in white as he pressed an illuminated button, "he will explain everything, oh and do watch your language when you speak to him, that grammar won't at all do."

"Uh, ok faggot." Skud replied as he walked into the elevator followed by the man.

The elevator was very luxurious with suede riveting, like one of those old timey ones, so Skud immediately knew he wasn't at a police station.

There were a whole bunch of standard elevator buttons, but the man pushed the one at the very top and it lit up marked P. The elevator started moving and Skud used his hoodie sleeve to wipe his face some more while the man in white pulled a pocket watch on a chain out of his vest to check the time. DING! The doors to the elevator slid open to reveal a hallway made almost completely of marble with a high vaulted ceiling, a set of large double doors at the end.

"Right this way sir." Said the man in white, motioning with his arm for Skud to go first. Skud started walking out of the elevator and down the hallway, the man in white directly behind him. As he was walking, Skud noticed the art on the walls every couple of feet which was mostly extremely detailed paintings of biblical themes in golden frames, he was starting to realize where he was.

As the two men approached the massive double doors, the man in white spoke,

"I hope you know how lucky you are to be in the presence of salvation."

Grabbing both handles on the doors, the man in white swung the doors open to reveal a massive room with vaulted ceilings, columns and floors of marble and a massive window over-looking downtown. There was a desk in front of the massive central window where two men in black robes sat across from a man in a rotating big-backed leather chair, who was looking out the window. Skud could see it was daytime again. The man in white motioned Skud forward and as he started walking in towards the other men, he could hear one of the two men in robes speaking in an accent.

"Ve haf been doing our job for years, it iz time for you to do the same" he said as he got up from his seat and gestured to the other man in black robes, "Let's go Heinrich."

The two men turned around and walked briskly out of the "office" past Skud and the man in white, who was holding one of the two doors open for them.

Still looking out of the window, the man in the chair spoke,
"Sometimes the world isn't enough for some people, ahh but I digress."

Now spinning the chair around, a man in an even more immaculate suit with even more vibrant blonde hair and brighter eyes than the man who led Skud in.

"Please have a seat my son, we have much to discuss" the man said, standing up and gesturing for Skud to take one of the newly vacated seats, which he did.

"So, hey man wh—" Skud started in but before he could finish the man put his hand up to halt him from speaking and addressed the first man in white who was still standing by the doors.

"That will be all Lucas, you are dismissed." The first man in white nodded and walked out of the room closing the doors behind him.

"You know, for such a dangerous guy you were pretty easy to apprehend, Skud" the man said now reaching his hand out across the desk to shake Skud's hand. "Samuel Alastair Young, but around here they address me as The Seer."

Skud shook the man's hand with regret now realizing where he was and who he was speaking to, the fucking seer of the Former Day Saints. These guys only had and cared about one agenda, theirs, and they went about fulfilling it by any means possible. Like Skud didn't already have enough shit to worry about, now he had these religious nut's attention and even worse he was in the office of their head honcho, just fucking peachy.

CHAPTER 10: THE LONG DICK OF THE LAW

Last night

"Ahhh another glorious night on the beat" Detective Moe Scheffield said as he got into the driver seat of his muscle car and turned the engine over. He lit a cigarette, put the car in drive and started off down the street away from Puss N' Boots and towards the police station to file his grisly report.

"When will this shit end" he said out loud to himself, taking a long thought out drag of his cigarette and turning the corner onto the street where the police station was.

Moe pulled around the back of the station and into "his spot." He got out of the car, dropped his cigarette on the ground, stepped on it and headed towards the back door of the station where he knew there was a newly orphaned little girl waiting for him to be interviewed. He let out a heavy sigh and walked through the door.

Detective Moe Scheffield was born and raised in Pepper-Mountain City and only ever thought about leaving once or twice in his life. He had quite the average childhood, two parent household, white picket fence and all that but in a city dying of an incurable disease. Growing up in Pepper-Mountain City Moe was able to see first-hand the rapid degradation of his home through rampant drug use, organized crime, legalized prostitution, political corruption, and a seemingly unregulated religious government. By the time he was in high school the city had gotten so bad that his parents moved to the suburbs to get Moe out of the nightmare it was to become. Not being one to stand on the sidelines he decided that he wanted to be a police officer, a dream which he fulfilled. Right out of the academy Moe was thrust onto the streets of a murderous city, a city with at least 6 homicides a day- by the time he became detective it was down to only 5. The department put Moe on all of the grisliest cases from day one, which you would think would have developed a strong stomach... something he still lacked.

About 2 months into Moe's tenure as a police officer he responded to a call that came over the radio for a domestic disturbance but when he got there it wasn't just some argument. The scene Moe walked into is something he still wakes up in the middle of the night over, even after everything he's seen since then. When Moe arrived at the scene and walked up to the door, he heard a woman screaming and crying, begging a shouting man to not do something, and then a gunshot! He kicked through the door, heard another gunshot and shouted "Police! Drop your weapon!"

He heard a woman scream for help from the next room over and when he turned the corner, he saw a man with a revolver holding a woman with the gun pressed to her head and two dead little kids on the floor next to them. Before Moe could even react, the man shot the woman in her head, sending skull fragments and brain matter across the room! Stunned, Moe shot and then kept shooting the man until his gun was clicking, spent of ammunition. This moment was forever seared into Moe's head and no matter how many medals of accommodation and promotions he got he could never erase it.

Thus was the beginning of Moe Sheffield's career as a homicide detective. His superiors gave him a medal of accommodation for his bravery, even though he didn't save anyone's life but his own and transferred him to the homicide division.

After a few years and a few more medals Moe was a staple of the Pepper-Mountain city homicide unit, known for his brutal interrogations of suspects. Moe found the best way to get answers from criminals was to beat them senseless, which he did regularly, but this time his only witness was an innocent little child, this would require a softer touch.

Walking through the hallways of the police station

and towards the interrogation room, Moe was hit with an all too familiar scent, the same scent that all prisons and hospitals have, institution. Rounding the last hallway corner before his destination, the detective saw two women in matching pant suits accompanied by who he recognized as Sue Heckler, the social worker assigned to the department.

"Hey Sue!" Moe shouted to her as he got closer, "aren't you a sight for sore eyes."

But instead of being greeted by her usual warmth, Sue simply put her hand in the air with her finger up, as if to tell Moe to wait. Slightly confused, the detective kept walking towards the women until he was close enough to hear what they were saying.

"I just don't understand why you think that this girl needs to be removed from our custody, we haven't even had a chance to find out if she has somebody!!" said Sue, "I don't know who gave you that authority!"

The older of the two women replied, "Ma'am we appreciate everything you are trying to do here but the authority of our organization supersedes any earthly authority, we are taking the child."

"Listen here bit-" Sue started in but before she

could continue Moe interrupted,

"Hey now ladies let's relax for a second, I'm sure we can come to a solution, no need for the hostility" he turned to the older of the two women,

"Now miss…."

"Mrs. Hathaway" the woman responded,

"Mrs. Hathaway, this little girl has been through a lot, and I know you folks run a fine facility over there, but would it be too much for me to just ask her a few questions? It won't take but five minutes. Is that ok ma'am?" Moe said.

The woman stood silent for a few seconds and then finally replied with, "Well I suppose, seeing as you asked me so nicely, unlike this little harlot accompanying you, do try and be quick."

"Thank you, ma'am" Moe replied, "Sue, take a walk."

Detective Moe Scheffield exhaled and opened the door to the interrogation room. He walked in and saw the little girl, sitting in the chair usually reserved for criminals, with a sad and empty look in her eyes and a gray blanket over her shoulders. Moe took his seat across from the little girl and started to speak, "Hey honey, I'm detective Moe Scheffield, what's your name?" No reply. He tried again, "Sweetheart I know it's hard, but I really need you to tell me some stuff ok? It's important."

With a slight sniffle the little girl looked up at Moe,

"Its… Its Christina" she said.

"Oh Christina! What a beautiful name for such a beautiful girl," Moe said, "I want you to do something for me sweetie, as hard as it is, I want you to tell me what happened tonight, ok?"

The girl let out a cry and slumped her head onto the table, "It's ok sweetie, please just one time. I need you to tell me who you saw" Moe pleaded with the little girl, "I want to find them and save your mommy." The little girl raised her head and wiped some tears from her eyes,

"Well, sniffle I went to work with mommy like I do sometimes, and I was in the back playing with the girls until they had to go out and dance."

"Ok, good and then what Christina" Replied Moe. The little girl continued.

"I was playing with mommy's friend Chantelle until she had to go work and then I was alone in the back trying on wigs when I started hearing loud pops and screams so I hid in a locker." She started to sniffle some more but continued on, "then the pops and screaming stopped and mommy's boyfriend came running into the back room"

Moe interrupted, "Mommy's boyfriend? Who is mommy's boyfriend?" Christina sat silent for a second and then looked at Moe and casually said,

"Mommy's boyfriend is the funny man, Skud."

The door to the interrogation room sprung open and Mrs. Hathaway started walking in with the other woman, towards the little girl and detective.

"Well Christina it was a pleasure, these two nice ladies are going to take you to a place with other little kids and lots of toys, behave yourself" Moe said as he got up from his seat, having got what he wanted, a name. He walked past the two ladies, "Ma'am" he said, nodding his head with respect and out the door back into the hallway.

Moe held the door open for the two ladies as they walked the little girl out of the room hearing Mrs. Hathaway say, "Oh how lucky for you my child, the day of your salvation has arrived." They continued walking down the hallway towards the door to the lobby and when they got to the door the little girl looked back at Moe with a sad look in her eyes and waved.

"I need a cigarette." He said out loud to himself and started walking the other way towards the back door. Moe pulled a cigarette from his pack and put it to his lips as he inched toward the door but before he got there someone shouted for him from down the hallway,

"Moe! You better come quick, they found some dead grease-ball bookie across town." Moe pulled the cigarette from his lips and put it back into his pack,

"Fan-fucking-tastic" he said and started walking towards the officer.

CHAPTER 11: AIM FOR THE BUSHES

Skud gulped quietly as he let go of the Seer's hand and replied,

"It's an honor to meet you, sir."

The seer raised his eyebrow at Skud as he unbuttoned his blazer and put his hand on his hip, sitting on the edge of his desk.

"Why don't you cut the rubbish son?" he said to Skud, "We're way past the pleasantries by now." He continued, "I could sure use a drink" slapping his hands on his knees and getting up from the desk, "how about you boy?" making a finger gun at Skud.

"Uh, yeah sure man, you got any rum?" Skud replied, slightly confused, seeing as the Former Day Saints were fundamentally opposed to drinking, nonetheless, day-drinking. The "Seer" walked from his desk and across his "office" over to a modest, but well-stocked wet bar and grabbed two rocks glasses. There was a slight popping noise when The Seer opened an opaque green bottle with no label, he took a sniff from it and spoke,

"This, my dear boy, this is a bottle of spiced rum, salvaged from the wreckage of a pirate ship in the Caribbean, dated 1746, quite exquisite."

Skud's mouth was slightly salivating from his alcoholism after hearing the distinct sound of booze being poured into the glass. The Seer walked back over to Skud with two glasses, three fingers each, and handed one to him, "Do try to savor it."

Oh, the relief… from getting his ass kicked all morning Skud had forgotten about having the shakes, but boy did he ever. He grabbed the glass from the Seer's hand took a look at his medicine and drank it all in one gulp.

"Wow" he said, examining the empty glass in his hand, "that was exquisite." No more shakes. Skud paused for a moment to let the burning sensation subside and then continued, "I don't mean to be rude, like thanks for the booze and all, but I thought your kind didn't partake?" The Seer let out a sigh, looking into his glass of rum.

"You're right Skud, we don't, but today is a most joyous occasion you see" he swirled his glass around and then walked over to the window, his back to Skud. He stood silent for a second or two and then motioned for Skud to join him at the window. "Won't you come see my son." Even more confused but relaxed and warm from the rum, Skud got up out of his chair and walked to the window.

From the window Skud could see the whole Former Day saints complex that littered a whole section of the city, a hospital, an orphanage, a woman's shelter and the crown jewel of the Saints, The Tabernacle. All these buildings were in exquisite "Greco-Roman" style, including the houses.

"You see how much we have done for this city Skud?" the Seer said, "but yet, there is suffering in place of prosperity, hate in the place of love, death in the place of life…why do they not see the way, the truth, the light?" he continued. He turned and looked Skud directly in his eyes, "I'll tell you why… FAITH, an extreme lack of faith!" he said, a thin layer glazing his eyes, "but you and me are going to change all of that aren't we?" So many thoughts raced through Skud's head but only one made it out of his mouth,

"What the hell are you talking about man? And where are my friends?" he asked.

The Seer walked over to his desk, put down his drink and turned back to look at Skud, who was still standing at the window, "Well why don't you take a look out that window towards the women's shelter?" Skud looked to the right and down a few stories at the women's shelter through the window.

"What am I looking for dude?" he said to the Seer and right after the words left his mouth he saw it, a black-haired woman who appeared to be struggling with someone near the top-right window, Layla. He pressed his hands against the glass and looked closer…He watched as Layla's body was flung from the top story window, her scream silent through his window as she dropped lower and lower and then…SPLAT!!! Looks like she lost the struggle. A normal person would've closed their eyes before she hit the ground, but not Skud, he had to see it.

"Jesus Chri—" Skud started but before he could finish the Seer slapped him right across his face, hard.

"NOT IN MY PRESENCE!!" he slapped him again, "EVER!" he yelled over top of Skud, who was now on the floor. Skud wiped some blood from his mouth and said with a chuckle, "Cheap shot" and leapt up towards The Seer to commence an ass whooping but was stopped by a gun in his face!

"Sit…down," The Seer said to Skud, now motioning the gun at him, "We have something to discuss." Skud, with his hands up, started walking back towards the chair.

"Look man, I don't know what's going on, but tempers got a little hot, I'm sitting" He said as he sat in the chair. The Seer spoke,

"I have no intention of killing you my son, but

make no mistake, I will act in self-defense," "Now—" he started in as he put the gun back in his jacket, "Where were we? Oh yes, you were going to retrieve my briefcase from your mob buddies." Now Skud was really confused.

"Look, with all due respect and remember I'm saying with all due respect, I'm not doing a fucking thing for you buddy, you dragged me in here, had your cult members rough me up and then killed one of my bitches, who do you think you are?"

"The only man who can keep you out of jail and keep your former associates from killing you" said The Seer as he slid a copy of today's newspaper in front of Skud.

POLICE SEEKING MAN IN CONNECTION WITH MULTIPLE HOMICIDES, LOCAL BOOK-MAKER AND EXOTIC DANCERS DEAD!

"Fuck me." said Skud, and that was just the headline, he kept reading...Long-time local bookmaker and known mafia affiliate Salvatore Cagliari, was found bludgeoned to death and with his heart removed in his residence in a suspected robbery... Police say the suspect, a man called Skud is wanted in connection with this murder and wanted for his connection to a violent shootout that occurred at a local gentleman's club leaving 7 dead. Police are asking anyone with information to come forward.

"Sal," Skud said softly as he shoved the paper back towards The Seer, thinking of his options, none, he had no choice but to hear this prick out. "So, what do you want?"

"Well, you see, Don Venetucci is in possession of a certain briefcase with a certain...book, shall we say. I need you to simply go over to the good ol' Don and retrieve it for me...and don't you worry I already took the liberty of calling Mr. Venetucci and explained to him how much of a misunderstanding this all is, he assures me you won't be harmed." Said The Seer.

Skud replied, "Why can't you just do it? You have like a thousand guys" The Seer spoke,

"Ah you see, this matter is of utmost importance to me, and I cannot be seen as to do business with the likes of the Don...besides I heard you possess special talents, talents I need, to mediate between me and scum like him."

"But the cops? and Layla, why the fuck did you do that?" said Skud.

"Oh that? That was for my man the other night, you know the one whose heart you ripped out in an alley and whose wife you fornicated with...

an eye for an eye I guess" replied The Seer, with cold indifference, "The police you need not worry about, I will simply tell them that you couldn't have committed those murders, seeing as you were interned at our rehabilitation facility for the past two weeks, they'll take my word, we only provide the majority of their funding, AFTER you get the briefcase."

Skud got up and walked over towards the wet bar where the Rum was and grabbed the bottle, "Just a briefcase huh? I'll do it, but I'm taking this" he popped open the top and looked at The Seer, "Cheers" he said and took a swig. Skud wiped his mouth and continued, "Oh and I need Thorne" he took another swig and wiped again, "He's my driver."

The Seer nodded his head and pressed a button on his intercom, "Miss. Clewell, could you send up the gentleman we have in room B225 and an escort for our guests?"

"Right away Sir" he walked away from the intercom, over to Skud and pulled a piece of paper out of his pocket, "You can drop the briefcase at this location" The Seer handed it to Skud,

"The old military base? Alright I guess." The base he was talking about was an old Russian base on the outskirts of the city, in the desert, the kids in town would go up there and party, get lost and all kinds of shit…as good a place as any he supposed.

The Seer ushered Skud towards the door as the same two men from the room downstairs opened it, "Well Skud, I've enjoyed our little tete-a-tete but I'm afraid I have a sermon to deliver, your friend will be in our back garage waiting, wouldn't want to be seen on the street right now- it's quite a mess" he pressed his intercom again "Miss. Clewell, please tell the women's shelter to put in those shatter-proof windows."

"Right away sir"

The Seer picked up his drink and called out, "Hey Skud!"

Skud turned around right as he got to the doorway,

"Cheers!" said The Seer as he downed the rum and put it down onto the now exposed sports' section of the paper… Opera win by 10 in shocking upset!! Skud scoffed and just kept walking.

OPERA WIN
BY 10

Chapter 12: When it Rains

Detective Moe Scheffield dropped his cigarette on the ground and stepped on it,

"Here we go again" he said as he walked through the front door of Sal's place. "Forced entry" he kept walking, "signs of a struggle, broken fish tank and—sweet Jesus!"

When the detective came upon Sal's corpse it wasn't pretty, his face was completely swollen and bloody and almost unrecognizable, his muscle shirt was completely stained in blood and the coup de gras, a cavity in his chest, with a heart missing.

"We got a name for the victim?" said Moe to one of the other officers on the scene.

"It's Salvatore Cagliari, sir" replied the officer, a stumpy white man.

"Cagliari? Mob guy, huh?" Moe said as he squatted down over top of the corpse and kept examining. He stayed in that position for a minute or two and then got up and walked over to a desk with a bunch of papers on it.

Moe started shuffling the papers around, a bunch of names, numbers, and gambling slips among various sporting teams, info. A name was circled on one of the gambling slips, Skud, the detective picked it up and put it in his pocket.

"Call the station, tell them we got our man." He spoke.

Moe looked for anything else that might be a clue in the kitchen but all he found were some dirty dishes and empty beer bottles, "Tape the area off and get the coroner down here, contact next of kin and all that jazz, I think it's time I paid the don a visit and ask him why all his guys are dying."

He said to the stumpy officer as he pulled out a cigarette and put it in his mouth. He continued as he took his first long drag, "That's gonna' have to wait until tomorrow though, I've had enough of this shit tonight, I'm going home."

The engine of Moe's muscle car roared as he took off down the street and home, he turned up the radio in his car, Truth of The Nation by D.O.D, he loved that song. Singing along and smoking his bogey he got to thinking, much like he always did on his way home.

"The heart thing is…weird" he said out loud to himself, "reminds me of that guy from a few years back, but I caught that guy" he continued and flicked his cigarette out the window, he was talking of course about THE GRAVESMASHER.

"The Grave Smasher" was a name the press coined for a brutal serial killer a few years back in Pepper-Mountain city, who terrorized the town. It all started with a body found next to a destroyed headstone in a graveyard. As it would turn out the victim's name matched the name on the headstone, this trend occurred for weeks, body after body, each murder grislier than the others, no leads…Until Moe Scheffield got on the case.

When the first body was found, Moe was up to his eyeballs in paperwork, but by the time the 6th body was found, the captain came to him directly. Moe got put on the case and immediately noticed similarities between the victims, all of them had a vital organ removed. It was the same guy in his mind. For the next few nights Moe ordered men from the homicide division to stake out all of the cemeteries in town, nothing until one night…He decided to take the old north end cemetery as his stake out point and boy did it pay off, at around 3 am he saw it, a shadowy figure dragging a body into the cemetery. Moe Scheffield jumped out of his car and started running towards the figure,

"Freeze Motherfucker!" he shouted as he drew his gun down on the perp, the now visible man in all black took off running.

Moe let off three shots at the man, but they all

missed, two hitting headstones the man ran behind, "Damn it!" he said out loud as he started running after the man but then he felt a burning pain in his chest, "What the fuck?" he clutched his hand to his chest, a knife, the fucker somehow threw a knife into Moe. He pulled out his radio, "Officer down, backup."

For the next few weeks out of the hospital Moe had been receiving letters from the Grave-Smasher, taunting letters with vague clues and victim's names. He still had the knife he got stabbed with and had been examining it non-stop and couldn't get anything from it, no prints, nothing until he was out to eat at a restaurant and saw the same type of knife on his table. Moe started keeping an eye on the restaurant, Lil Ho Phuc's, every night, especially this one guy, the dishwasher. This dishwasher fit the bill, he had long-greasy black hair, wore all black with pentagrams and eyeliner. This went on for days, it was personal for Moe, this prick stabbed me, an obsession bore fruit eventually when he followed the dishwasher on a Friday night…

There was this goth club the dishwasher went every night, but he always left alone and went home. Not tonight though, tonight he had company. A young lady who looked about the same age as the dishwasher. Moe watched as they walked down the street and towards a park, he pursued on foot. He stood behind a tree, careful not to be seen, as the two walked closer to some benches under a gazebo, it looked like they were kissing. Moe looked away; public displays of affection made him uncomfortable, too bad for the young lady. Moe heard a scream, he popped from behind the tree and saw the dishwasher standing over top of the young woman, he ran towards the two and shot, this time he didn't miss, right in the guy's shoulder.

"Stay on the ground you son of a bitch! I'll blow your fucking head off" he said to the dishwasher with his gun pointed at him, the girl was still alive, thank God, just a bite taken out of her neck.

"What the fuck dude?" said the dishwasher, clutching his shoulder and whimpering. Moe kicked him right in his face.

"Shut the fuck up!" he shouted as he violently handcuffed the young man, "Let's go" Moe lifted the dishwasher off of the ground and started dragging him towards his car and threw him in the trunk.

After 3 days in the trunk with severe intermittent beatings, the dishwasher confessed to being the Grave- Smasher to the detective after days of insisting he wasn't, and Moe Scheffield got another medal.

"That had to be the guy, the killings stopped after that" Moe said out loud as he started driving towards the FDS part of the city. He liked to drive that way home instead of the overpass, the architecture made him feel at ease, the sun was up now and the gleaming off of the marble buildings was sublime.

"Ahh, at least the whole city isn't ugly" Moe said as he took out another cigarette from his pack and lit it.

Now getting closer to the Tabernacle, he sighed a sigh of relief, taking a long drag from his cigarette and stopping at the intersection stoplight.

"Beautiful!" he said out loud looking forward, truly relaxed, people walking down the street on their ways to work, as he closed his eyes to breathe it in, he was interrupted by the sound of screams. He opened his eyes and saw people looking up, screaming and sighing and then he saw why, a woman was falling from a high story building and right into the concrete a few yards from his car... Moe closed his eyes and took a long drag from his cigarette, "Jesus, it never ends" he exhaled....

CHAPTER 13 : COMPOUNDED INTEREST

So, there was Skud and Thorne in the Former-day Saints underground garage, getting back into the Tahoe. Thorne got into the driver's seat and started the engine, Skud into the passenger seat, the garage doors opened, and they were off.

"Take a right" Skud said to Thorne, knowing that if they went left, they would run into the police and Thorne might crack at the sight of Layla's splattered corpse on the ground.

They went right. Thorne started in,

"So uh, hey man, what the hell was that all about?" he continued, "I know you and me ain't the most savory guys but that was a little much…fucking Former Day Saints? What type of shit are you into Skud?"

"Really not a big deal, honestly the dude just wants me to go grab his briefcase from the don," Skud said as he pulled out a cigarette and lit it, "A lot of fucking theatrics if you ask me." he continued as he took a long drag, "But the way I see it, I gotta' walk to the don anyway, me and him got some shit to sort out, go left up here."

Thorne replied, "But that's not the way to—" Skud interrupted,

"I know bro, I know…I wanna' cruise by Sal's place

first, let's go."

As they rounded the corner, Skud could see there weren't any cops out front of Sal's place, but he told Thorne to pull around the back just in case. They pulled into the alley and parked about 3 houses down from Sal's, "Wait here." Said Skud as he opened the door and flicked his cigarette, "You see anybody come towards the house, you just get the fuck out of here alright?" he said and then walked off down the alley towards Sal's back door.

Skud walked carefully and quietly as he approached Sal's place, he quietly opened the gate, and went to the back door. He twisted the knob… it was open, and walked in. Even though it was a relatively nice day, it was pitch-black inside of Sal's, except for some rays of sunlight coming through the windows. Police tape was up all around the place and Skud could see that there was some sort of fight in there, broken shit everywhere, blood stains on the floor. He really didn't care about any of that, what he cared about was the secret gun stash Sal had hopefully the police didn't find it. Skud walked lightly to the living room and stopped at the broken fish tank,

"Ah man, poor fuckin fish" he said and kept walking towards Sal's recliner where he knew the gun safe was in a secret compartment under the rug.

Skud got to the front of the chair and lifted up the rug, "Yes!" he said to himself out loud when he saw the false floor planks were still there. He lifted the planks and saw the safe, "Bingo!"

Skud went to start putting in the combination and he heard the back door open, then footsteps, so he threw the rug down over the safe and hid behind the recliner. The footsteps were slow and steady, getting closer and closer and then the man spoke,

"I saw you come in here you little prick!" Skud then heard an all too familiar sound, a gun cocking. He stayed behind the recliner silent, he looked around, the only way out was a window on the other side of the living room, looks like he was gonna' have to fight his way out.

The man walked closer and closer to the recliner, Skud could hear the footsteps growing louder and louder, he waited for his moment. He sat there silently, breathing lightly and then he saw the man's hand with a gun come around the chair to his right side, his moment had arrived. Skud kicked the man's hand, and the gun flew across the room, he leapt up and swung with his left hand, delivering a hard uppercut. The man stumbled back and into one of the beams of light shining through, he was slightly taller than Skud and more muscular, with short, slick-backed black hair and eyeliner.

"Oh, you wanna' do this the hard way huh?" said the man, "I'm gonna' enjoy this!" he continued as he removed the outer jacket of his suit and tossed it on the floor, rolling up his sleeves.

"Let's dance motherfucker!" shouted Skud as he lunged forward.

Skud swung a haymaker with his left hand, which was immediately caught by the other man, who delivered a hard ass headbutt right to the center of Skud's face and then 3 equally hard punches in a row. That one hurt. Skud stumbled back and tried again, but this time the man caught his arm and judo flipped him through the coffee table in the middle of the room. Laying there with the wind knocked out of him, Skud stared up at the ceiling, thinking how much that just hurt when his vision was blocked by a dress-shoed foot coming straight for his face. Skud snapped out of it, quickly rolled to the left and sprung onto his feet, just narrowly avoiding his curtain call.

Now standing next to the man, Skud delivered a hard chop to his throat and then a right hook right to the center of his face. The man stumbled back gripping his throat with his right hand.

"Now you're really gonna' fuckin' pay!" The other

man said as he collected himself back into a fighting stance.

The man ran forward and started swinging, left hook, blocked, right hook, blocked, shin kick, avoided and then another right hook, BOOM! The punch connected, Skud stumbled back, bleeding now, but still in the fight he pressed his attack. He led with a perfectly executed right roundhouse kick aimed at the man's head, which to Skud's chagrin he caught with both of his hands, "Fuck?"

The man dropped an elbow into Skud's inner thigh, sending a searing pain down his whole leg. Skud started to let out a scream, but it was cut short when the man grabbed the back of his hoodie and tossed Skud into the wall face first. With his head in the wall, Skud was dazed and had drywall in his mouth, the taste was awful, it tasted like drywall, and you know… nut-sack.

Skud pulled his head out of the wall and before he could spit out the drywall, it was punched out of his mouth by another right hook, problem solved. After the hook, Skud fell to his knees, blood running out of the side of his mouth, the man gripped the left side of Skud's hair and started punching him in the face repeatedly and hard. Blood spattered with each punch and after 6 or 7 Skud was ready to check out. He couldn't really see the guy's face because of how dark it was, which was a shame because Skud would really like to look into the eyes of the man who was about to take his life.

"Any last words you piece of shit?" the man said to Skud, holding him by the collar with his fist cocked back,

"Yeah!" he said as he spit all the blood in his mouth into the man's face, making him flinch, giving Skud a split second to deliver the world's hardest nut punch straight to the dude's balls, which he did.

"Shoulda' worn a cup."

Skud headbutted the man, he stumbled back and Skud started swinging, he landed 5 punches to the man before his sixth one was caught again. The man pulled Skud in by his arm and got him in a choke hold,

"You really are a slippery little bastard" he said as his forearms tightened around Skud's throat, "Time to die."

Skud clawed at the man's forearms, but it did nothing, closer and closer to death Skud's vision started to fade,

"No, not like this" he said to himself as he gripped

both of the man's forearms and flipped him over his head and right onto his back on the floor! Skud stumbled over to where the man lay on the floor, Skud stumbled over to where the gun had landed and picked it up. He turned around to draw down on the man, but the man was already there, he grabbed Skud's wrist and started twisting so Skud started firing but none of the bullets hit the man, click, click, empty.

Skud dropped the gun, kneed the man in the stomach and dropped a hammer fist to the back of the man's neck, his body went limp. With the man now lying face down on the floor, Skud let out a sigh and started walking back towards the gun safe but was tripped by the man who apparently wasn't dead, now gripping him by the ankle.

"Fuck you, you motherfucker" the man said to Skud, laying on his stomach, blood covering his face.

Skud started kicking the man in his face with his other foot until the man let go. Now enraged, Skud jumped up off of the ground, grabbed the man who was face down by the back of his collar and waistline and started dragging him towards the broken fish tank. When they got to the fish tank, Skud grabbed the man by the back of his hair and cocked his head back.

"Time for you to die" Skud said as he drove the mans cocked back head down onto the broken edge of the fish tank, throat first.

The sound of gurgling blood filled Skud's ears with pleasure and it sent him into a blind euphoric rage.

"Not so tough now huh?" he said out loud as he started moving the man's head back and forth on the broken glass until his head was in Skud's hand. He held it up to see the man's face finally and it was his face. His head!

"What the fuck?" Skud said as he dropped the head to the floor and walked into the kitchen and opened the fridge. He grabbed a beer, cracked it open and chugged it. "Cheers Sal" he said out loud as he finished the beer and dropped the bottle to the floor.

CHAPTER 14: SCREAM BLOODY GORE

The passenger door to the Tahoe flung open and there stood Skud, blood running from his nose and mouth,

"Jesus man, what the hell happened to you?" Thorne said as Skud tossed an Ak-47 into the backseat. Opening a box of ammunition and loading bullets into a banana-clip magazine, Skud replied,

"Well, you see Thorne, seems like the good old Don has some type of death wish" chick-cuh he cocked the gun and continued "I'm going to oblige him."

Thorne's eyes widened, "Are you fucking nuts?" Skud chuckled and pulled a beer out of his pocket and handed it to Thorne,

"Here, ya pussy. Relax a little bit, just drop me off there…and Thorne, you know I'm fucking nuts!"

Thorne sighed and put the car in gear, "Alright man, whatever you say" and they were off towards the compound.

DING! The elevator doors opened, and Moe Scheffield was being led into the Seer's office by the man in the white suit.

"Detective! How blessed! Please, please have a seat and get comfortable." The Seer said, smiling from behind his desk all the while. Moe sat down. The Seer leaned forward and asked,

"Would you like a drink, detective? We have an exquisite selection for our esteemed guests."

Moe replied, "No, don't touch the stuff, thank you your grace."

The Seer leaned back and folded his hands, "Ah good man…Now detective, to what do I owe this pleasure?" Moe pulled out his notepad and hunched forward,

"Well, you see your grace, It's been a particularly brutal night and day and I've had to deal with some pretty gruesome stuff"

The seer nodded and opened his hands, "I'm sorry for that my son, please continue." Moe continued,

"Yeah thanks, it's no big deal, pretty typical for a night in the city, but what isn't too typical is why I got a couple of dead mob guys wearing your suits, coincidence?"

The Seer looked at the detective's face, smiled, got up from his chair and walked towards the window. Looking out he spoke, "Do you love this city detective?"

Moe replied, "Born and raised her sir, love it, but

my question?" The Seer continued,

"I love this city, so much so in fact we operate a multitude of charitable facilities."

Scheffield interrupted, "Yeah I know, saw the girl down below, so sad."

"Yes, truly a tragedy, one that will be avoided in the future due to our new windows we are having installed, but that's a subject for another day." The seer turned from the window and started walking back towards the desk, he sat and continued, wiping a tear from his eye, "The men in the suits, detective, were a part of one of our programs aimed to help convicted criminals reform their lives' more than likely, I suppose these men fell victim to their old ways?"

No shit? Of course, that's why they had the, suits Moe thought to himself as he sat there scribbling some notes,

"Well seems to all check out your grace, terribly sorry if I wasted your time, I know you're a busy man" he said as he rose up from his seat and extended his hand to shake the Seer's.

"Not at all detective" The Seer started in as he gestured the detective towards the door, "Always glad to help rid the city of evil doers, which reminds me, what do you make of this whole Skud character?" Moe tuned and looked towards the Seer,

"Well, that's who I think has been killing all these guys. Know anything about him?" The seer opened the door to his office and answered,

"Well from what you just told me I'd say he has some type of vendetta with the mob…if you hurry, you just might catch him" he said to Moe as he left the office.

SCCUURTT!! The Tahoe screeched to a halt in the parking lot of the Venetucci Mob Compound,

"Alright man, shit's gonna' get real ugly in there, you should probably take off" Skud said to Thorne as he hopped out of the vehicle and grabbed the AK-47.

Thorne looked at Skud and said, "You sure about this man? There's gotta' be at least 50 guys in there?"

"Oh, I'm fucking sure alright." Skud said as he flung the gun over his shoulder and lit a cigarette. Thorne sighed, "Well alright man, I'm gonna' go grab a 12 pack, split it with me later?" Skud took a deep drag from his cigarette and tossed it,

"You know it brother" he said while shaking Thorne's hand. Skud turned around and heard the

Tahoe pull away.

The Venetucci Compound was a 7-floor office building, built in the same fashion as most of Pepper-Mountain city, "Greco-Roman". Skud walked towards the entrance, let out a deep breath, gun in hand and kicked open the door. The first floor was a marble covered masterpiece with vaulted ceilings, straight ahead there was a desk with a male receptionist behind it and two of Gino's men in suits to either side of the desk. Skud immediately opened fire on the two men to the sides of the desk, making their bodies twitch from the bullets until falling to the ground. The man behind the desk jumped up with a handgun but Skud shot him right in the chest and ran forward towards him. The man lay on the ground clutching his chest wound, Skud jumped over the desk and shot the man three more times until he stopped moving. He grabbed a key card off of the man's lapel and looked over at a monitor screen on the desk that showed all of the security cameras. "Good" Skud said out loud while changing out his gun's magazine, "They don't know I'm here yet."

Skud jumped from behind the desk, walked over to the first dead goon's body and grabbed the pistol from out of his holster. He did the same with the other dead goon except only taking the magazine out of the gun and finding a fat sack of coke.

"Yoink" Skud said and walked to the elevator that was to the right of the desk. He used the key card to open the doors and got in the elevator. When the doors closed Skud paused for a moment and opened the bag of cocaine. He dumped the bag into his hand and put it to his face, SSSSSNNN-NNFFFFTT!!! Skud pressed the 1 elevator button and it started to move.........

DING! He let out a roar as the doors opened revealing a hallway with 3 men in suits. BLAT! BLAT! BLAT! BLLLLAATTTT!!! They all fell to the floor and Skud ran forward.

At the end of the hallway and to the right was a set of double doors, Skud kicked them open to reveal a small warehouse with people in face masks, aprons and hair nets, packaging up cocaine. Reggaeton music blared over a loudspeaker in the room and before the workers could even look up, Skud opened fire. Powder flew up in the air in all directions, the workers scrambled to find cover, all but one failed, a woman. He walked towards her, cocaine falling on his shoulders and all around him like a snowstorm, gun in hand. The woman was crouched behind a stack of kilos, crying, muttering in Spanish.

"Shhh, esta bien, go home your free." Skud said to her as he helped her up. Skud walked in front of her towards a door to a stairwell and then he heard some feet shuffling and next thing you know there was a knife his back, literally…the woman had stabbed him in the right shoulder.

"Ahhh! You fucking bitch!" Skud said as he turned around, delivering a vicious punch to the woman and then immediately shooting her twice.

He pulled the knife from his shoulder, letting out a scream as it came out,

"Fuck man" Skud said as he tossed the knife to the floor and touched the wound. He walked over to one of the tables with a pile of blow on it, grabbed another handful and ripped it, rubbing the excess on his hand on the newly acquired stab wound. Skud let out a roar like a lion and ran full sprint up the staircase towards the sixth floor, he'd deal with the other floors later.

The sixth floor is where all of Gino's goons hung out, playing cards, smoking etc. Without stopping, Skud burst through the stairwell door to the sixth floor with his shoulder, the door hitting the guard behind it, knocking him to the floor. Five men sat at a card table to the right while two men were guarding a door on the other side of the room. The five men flipped the table as Skud opened fire from his AK-47 in their direction.

click click click

Skud bashed the man he had knocked over with the door on the head with the gun before dropping it and pulling out the pistol he had acquired in the lobby. He ran and leapt over the bar that was to the left as gunshots whizzed all around him.

With bullets flying over his head Skud took a deep breath and let out another roar as he jumped up from his cover. He aimed and shot the two men by the door, and they fell to the floor. The men from behind the table were firing handguns at Skud, he ducked behind the bar again. Skud looked around the bar until he found a bottle of grain alcohol, "Bingo!" he said out loud as he opened the bottle and took a swig and then started pouring some of the bottle onto a bar rag. Skud stuffed the rag into the bottle and pulled out his lighter, "Hey cocksuckers!" he yelled as he lit the rag, popping up from behind the bar, Molotov cocktail in hand, "Catch!" and then fast balled the flaming bottle to the wall behind the table where the men were crouched. Direct hit! Flames erupted and the men leapt up, all now engulfed by them. Skud started shooting and hit four of the flamers, but left one alive, to burn.

With no time to admire his artistry, Skud jumped

from behind the bar, ran past the flames and to the door. Gun in hand, he ran up the steps to the 7th floor, which he knew was just one long ass hallway to the Don's office at the end. Skud stopped at the door leading to the hallway at the top of the stairwell,

"Showtime" he said and ripped open the door.

A guard with his back turned stood right in front of Skud and about fifteen more scattered through the length of the hallway. He grabbed the man with his right hand around the neck, chokehold style, and pumped two shots into his back with the gun in his left hand.

One of the men down the hallway yelled, "HE'S HERE!" and they all drew their weapons. Skud kept a hold of the man and pushed forward, bullets rattled the human shield. Two of the bullets had managed to hit Skud in the arms, but he kept his composure, barely feeling them from the adrenaline and cocaine, and then…clicks, all empty guns.

Skud still held the man's lifeless body in his hand, the bullet wounds throbbing in his arms, he needed a boost to fight all fifteen of these fucks. Skud really hated to do this, but desperate times call for desperate measures and all that, so he reached his left hand back and thrust it through the man's chest, grabbing his heart. He dropped the man's body to the ground as the goons stormed towards him and took a bite from the warm flesh of the heart. His eyes widened as the blood ran down his throat, followed by muscley heart tissue and he dropped the heart to the ground.

Now embodied with the strength of another man, the bullet wounds healed, and the adrenaline flowed, Skud felt great. The first set of goons arrived, two of them, one to his left and one to his right, Skud shot the first man to the right and then the one to the left, click. The men fell to the floor, Skud ran forward, grabbing a goon by the face and smashing his head into the wall. Three more men charged Skud, he zipped the empty gun right into the first one's face, lodging it into his skull and then ran forward with a dropkick into the other two, knocking them to the ground. Skud sprung up from his side, immediately jumped onto one of the men and dug his thumbs into his eye sockets. He then hammer-fisted the other man on his back, crushing his face.

CRACCKK!! A kick landed to the side of Skud's head, and he fell to his back. He rolled out of the way as a stomp aimed for his head dropped and then smashed his elbow into the ankle, rendering it sideways.

"Gahhhh!!" the man let out a shriek as Skud leapt to his feet, grabbed the man's head and bashed it into an approaching goon's forehead. He ran past the recently felled henchmen towards the remaining seven, all charging him. WHAPP!! Throat chop to goon on the right, right hook to the left one, chest kick to the middle goon. One of the men swung a bat, which Skud rapidly caught with his left hand, then headbutting the man in the center of the face. Skud rammed the butt of the bat into one of the other men's faces and then swung it in an upward motion into the other man's chin…one left.

The final goon shuffled backwards in the direction of the office door, Skud had one final ace up his sleeve. He reached into his crotch as the goon rolled his sleeves up, the fear evident in his eyes, and pulled out a parting gift from Sal, a Grenade! Skud ran forward as he pulled the pin out of the grenade, the man frozen with shock,

"You're fuckin crazy man!!!" shouted the goon.

With the grenade in his left hand, Skud cocked his fist back and punched the grenade through the goon's teeth and into his mouth. Skud stepped back and kicked the goon in the chest, sending him through the door his back was now pressed against and into the Don's office. The man's head exploded as he flew through the door back first, sending shrapnel into the Don as he cowered behind his desk.

"You fucking prick!!" shouted the don, "Couldn't you just fucking knock?"

Skud took a step over the headless goon and towards the don, who was leaning on the floor behind his desk, clutching his chest.

"Where's my briefcase Gino?" Skud said as he ran his right hand down his face, wiping the blood, warpaint.

"That's what this is about?! For Fuck's sake Skud, I woulda' just given it to ya!" Gino replied. "Yeah, but we're way past the pleasantries aren't we you fuck?!" Skud said and lunged at the don, grabbing him by his collar.

He punched Gino in the mouth, hard, "WHY DID YOU SEND THOSE MEN TO KILL ME?!!"

The Don shuttered as the punch connected. Skud punched him again, knocking out teeth this time. The Don spoke,

"The men at the club…I sent them cause I thought you greased Sal, thought you finally snapped, that's it"

Skud punched the don in the face again, "You lying sack of shit" another punch, this one to the nose.

"Alright, alright…listen, the saints…they're planning something big…don't know what, all I know is they paid me a lot of fucking clams for this briefcase and told me they wanted you out of the way…my guys had to whack a general in his house for this thing… "…I know we got a history and whatnot Skud but business is business, you should know that better than most people…but that's it, that's all I know…the briefcase is under the desk…now take me to a fucking hospital." Don Gino Venetucci said and then gestured towards the briefcase. Skud dropped the don and grabbed the briefcase. He stood up and said, "Well Gino you see, I'd love to help but you're bad for business, and you know," Skud said, delivering a stomp to the center of the don's face, "Business is business."

CHAPTER 15: TUBTHUMPIN'

The sounds of muffled gunshots filled Thorne's ears as he sat in the Tahoe, a sound he was all too familiar with, having served two tours in the "middle east".

"Come on Skud, I got a cold one for you" he said out loud to himself as he swigged from his beer can. Thorne left after dropping off Skud but came back, because hell who was he kidding, he was his only friend, and he couldn't just leave him to die. GLUG GLUG GLUG, Thorne finished off his beer and crushed the can, now brandishing a 9mm pistol in his hand.

The Tahoe door screeched as Thorne exited the driver's seat and he stepped onto the concrete, the gunshots had stopped. He took a deep breath, exhaled and said, "alright here we go" as he walked towards the door to the compound.

"Freeze scumbag!" Thorne heard shouted from behind him, "Drop the weapon!" He turned around slowly and saw a man standing there, blonde hair and trench coat, aiming a gun at him. Thorne spoke,

"Ok man, be easy" as he started to put his gun down only to be interrupted by a door swinging open behind him.

Skud burst through the door, drenched in blood,

briefcase in hand and saw the two men. He assessed the situation and quickly realized what was happening, this was a cop, he turned to Thorne, "Run!" and they both bolted towards the Tahoe.

"I said freeze dammit!" Moe Scheffield shouted as he squeezed the trigger of his service revolver, letting off three shots at Skud and Thorne, missing as they leapt into the SUV.

"Go! Go! Go!" Skud shouted to Thorne as he put the vehicle in gear. ERRRRRTTTT!!! The tires screeched as they accelerated towards the detective. BOOM! BOOM! BOOM! Moe shot three more times and jumped out of the way, narrowly avoiding getting run over.

"Damn!" he said out loud and ran back to his car to get on the radio, "Dispatch, shots fired! Two male suspects…fleeing in vehicle…white SUV, Tahoe!" The detective hopped in the driver's seat of his muscle car to pursue. The engine roared as he put the pedal to the metal in hot pursuit, "Dispatch! In pursuit of suspects, heading north!"

"Fuck man! Was that a cop?!" Thorne said to Skud as he raced through the street.

Skud replied, "I think so dude, drive to the old missile base as fast as you can, take the backroads." He looked behind and saw a muscle car in the distance gaining on them, fast. "Step on it bro, we got company."

They drove at full speed, through the open red canyon spaces, towards the old missile base, Moe gaining on them rapidly.

"Hand me that gun" Skud said and gestured to Thorne, to which Thorne complied. He could see that the detective was almost in firing range, so he cocked the gun back and aimed out of the passenger window. BOOM! BOOM! BOOM! He let off three shots at Moe Scheffield's car, two hitting the hood.

"You mother—" the detective said out loud, putting his gun out the window, firing some shots of his own, blowing out the back window of The Tahoe. Thorne swerved as the shots hit the truck,

"Fuck! Fuck! Fuck!" he said, straightening the Tahoe back out.

"Just a couple of minutes man" Skud said to Thorne before reaching back out the window and firing four more shots at the detective, blowing out a headlight and missing the rest.

The pursuit continued for a few more minutes until Skud could see the run-down gate of the base in the distance.

"Almost there man, almost there" he said to Thorne and looked up.

Moe Scheffield held the wheel with his left hand and aimed his gun at his windshield. CREEESSH-HH!! He fired a shot, blowing out the windshield, thus giving himself better visibility and control.

"Alright you degenerate, this is over" he said aiming his revolver out of the broken windshield. Moe took a deep breath, closed one eye and let off a shot…missed…he took another deep breath and shot…BOOM! Direct hit to the back left tire, the Tahoe started swerving.

"Oh shit man, this isn't good" Thorne said while frantically trying to regain control of the vehicle, "Hold on!!"

The Tahoe swerved to left, then to the right and then… Thorne lost control and the car began to roll…

"Fuck" Skud said to himself. The Tahoe viciously rolled into a complete tumble, rolling a multitude of times and even going airborne until slamming to a halt upside down!

Ringing, nothing but ringing, that's all Skud could hear, he had blood in his eye, so he could only half see. He looked to his left and saw Thorne's mangled body lying motionless in the driver's seat. His bloody eye burned as the tears started to flow,

"Thorne…" he said softly. Closing his eyes, he took a deep breath in and then opened them, "Time to go" he said.

Skud crawled through the passenger window on his stomach, clutching the briefcase in his left hand and then standing up. The muscle car came to a stop about 15 feet away from Skud, he looked and without hesitation, took off running towards the gate.

Moe Scheffield ran over to the now destroyed SUV and looked in the driver's side,

"Rest in peace scumbag" he said while pulling Thorne's corpse from the wreckage. Moe dragged the body away from the smoking truck, walked over to his car and got on his police radio, "Dispatch… one suspect dead, other fleeing on foot, send backup to the old Russian missile base… I'm going in."

Skud kept running until he got to an old hatch that he knew led inside the base. Surrounded by high desert plains all around him, he opened the hatch and climbed down the ladder, THUD! Skud landed on the ground, slightly wet. There were lights on down the hallway, so he knew somebody was home.

"That fucking cop man, he killed Thorne" Skud said out loud to himself, did he? Or did you…? He heard echo in his head. He kept walking, following the hallway into a room with rows of large glass containers filled with clear liquid on each side and…something else.

"Holy mother of God…what the hell is this?" Skud said, looking at the containers, appalled. They were 7-foot-tall glass "test tubes" filled with a clear goo and…people. He looked at the first one on the right and it was the starting quarterback for BYU, next to him was the first lady of the United States, a congressman from Utah and a pop star. On the other side in the containers were, The Seer, a child he didn't recognize, The president of China and…himself?? Skud looked on in amazement,

"How? How could it be?" he continued, "I've finally fucking lost it."

THUNK!! The sound of the hatch closing echoed through the hallway and into the "vat-room", Skud snapped out of it and ran forward through the hallway on the other side of the room.

Following the trail of lights, the hallway opened up into another room, but this one had cages lined on the walls, filled with…children. Some of the children were silent, stunned, others cried and screamed for their mothers, Skud stood silent.

He walked slowly through the room, examining all the children's faces but only one caught his attention, a little girl with wide eyes, staring at him. "Christina?" he said softly to her, no reply, the girl just sat there with an empty look in her eyes as if there was nothing left.

"I'm gonna' get you out of here, I promise…. ALL OF YOU!" he shouted as he ran through the opposite doorway.

Skud kept walking down the hallway until he reached his destination, a massive command center, computers, flashing lights, a standing missile in the distance and a round table with men seated. One of the men stood up from the table, The Seer, he clapped his hands slowly three times,

"My my, I must say, I am thoroughly impressed with you Skud" he said. "Now if you don't mind, these men have been waiting for a very long time… my briefcase?" and motioned one of the other men towards Skud.

The man was in a black robe and had black beads hanging from the tunic, a Jesuit. Skud handed him the briefcase, the man bowed and walked briskly back to The Seer. His face lit up with joy as he opened the briefcase, like a kid on Christmas, "Ahh yes… finally… peace."

"Peace?" said Skud, "What about all those kids I just saw, and those tubes? What the fuck was all that?"

The Seer winced at the sound of the F word and then chuckled, "Oh you really are such a fool, oh how blind the sheep are even as the shepherd guides them home!"

Skud started to speak with his finger pointed at the Seer, "Look motherfucker, I want my name cleared, some money and some fucking an…. swer…. s." he felt a pinch in his neck and fell to the floor. Vision fading, he saw The Seer's footsteps drawing closer, "Answers, you shall have." …… darkness.

CHAPTER 16: THE FALL OF ROME

Breaking news! Hostage situation unfolding at Tekoi Rocket Test Range! Wanted murderer simply known as Skud has multiple prominent members of The Former Day Saints church underground! News televisions across the country all broadcasted a similar regurgitation. Swat teams mobilized as well as counter terrorists. The clock was ticking.

Skud saw his mom and dad standing happily together, smiling and kissing, he had to be fucking dreaming.

"Rise and shine" a faint voice spoke as the images disappeared and Skud woke up to The Seer lightly slapping his cheek. He went to rub his eyes but couldn't, his hands were bound to his sides, he was tied to something, but what? Still dazed from whatever this prick put in his neck,

Skud asked, confused, "What's going on? What is this?"

The Seer, standing on a metal floor, stairs behind him spoke, "This is your destiny my son…This is the cleansing."

The cleansing? Destiny? What was this guy talking about?

Shaking the daze off some more, Skud looked

around; he was standing straight up, The Seer directly in front of him, the men still seated at the table and the briefcase open next a man typing ferociously into an 80's computer. The Seer continued,

"You see Skud, the world we live in is dying from a rot that is so deep you can hardly tell right from wrong." He paced back and forth. "You, my son, are a prime example of this...How many people have you killed?" he asked Skud.

"I don't know man" Skud replied, the dried blood on his face now reconstituting from his sweat, "A bunch of no-good bastards, all of them though."

"Ahhhh, see, you fancy yourself as just while committing heinous crimes.... You aren't." The Seer prattled on, "I on the other hand, am just, you act on impulse, desire and all for the sake of your own preservation.... I on the other hand sit and wait, calculating, observing, maneuvering my pieces on the proverbial chess board until—" he was interrupted by the man typing on the computer, who was now finished, "The codes are in sir, waiting on you for launch."

The Seer smiled ear to ear, "Excellent work, to your places everyone."

Skud, now even more confused, spoke up, "Codes?

What codes, you fuckin nut?" He jerked his body a few times but to no avail, he was stuck.

Alastair, The Seer, replied, "Well today is your lucky day Skud, you get to be the hero you always thought you were…today you get to save the world"

save the world? Skud thought, what the fuck was this guy talking about. The Seer turned to face Skud and continued,

"You see, that thing you're tied to is an old two-stage rocket, you are on the first stage, the second stage is fitted with a nuclear warhead, one with enough payload to level a city…this city." What was left of Skud's heart dropped to his stomach,

"A nuke? Destroy the city? But why?" The Seer walked closer to him,

"Why? Are you stupid and blind? This city and all the others have become cesspools of depravation…just the way we wanted it—" Skud interrupted, angrily, "Who? Your little fuckin cult?" The Seer closed his eyes and opened them, revealing a set of lizard's eyes

"My little cult, as you say has done more for humanity than you could ever dream of and the people I answer to are far more aggressive than myself…So by we I mean our organization… you don't pay attention to the news, do you?" he blinked again, eyes returning to normal.

The Seer pulled his phone out and pressed play on a video, turning the screen to show Skud. The phone showed a newscast, a woman sat, stern, speaking,

"We are now receiving information that a terrorist known as Skud has access to a nuclear weapon and has intents to launch an attack, the US military is frantically trying to respond…God help us." he closed the video and put the phone away,

"As you can see, our friends in the media are playing their part." The Seer clasped his hand behind his back, turned around and spoke, "You are going to die tonight, a terrorist, and there is nothing that can stop it, fate and destiny are ours to control Skud and you, my son, have failed."

Tears now starting to well, Skud hung his head,

"So what? You're going to thwart my terroristic attempt and become a hero?" The Seer turned around, eyebrow raised,

"Thwart you? No, no, no…I mean to see the attack through." He stepped forward until he was face to face with Skud, a sinister look in his eyes, "Me and my colleagues here are all representatives of an organization that is nameless, faceless…well has many faces rather, but none you would recognize…so I'll tell you as a parting gift."

The Seer turned and spread his arms out towards the men at the table,

"The two men to your left are from The Jesuit Order…The man to their right is the highest-ranking member of The Vril society, a Nazi, and to his right is The Chief Rabbinate of Israel…The two men on his right are from the US Department of State." He continued, "For the past three hundred years, me and men like this have been working together to instill hatred and evil among humanity, through religion, propaganda, lies and force, poisoning all of your food, and when things get to a boiling point, we simply tear it down and start again… something we will be doing…tonight."

The Seer continued his speech, "That briefcase you brought me, it had some old nuclear launch codes in it that our friends from the State Department so generously gifted the don…the fool." Skud looked up, a stream of tears running down his cheeks,

"So, all of this…all of this pointless shit for me to bring you some codes?" The Seer interrupted,

"No, it wasn't pointless at all you see…after we destroy Pepper-Mountain City, the country will fly into panic, we'll launch another missile in your name, until the people will have nowhere to turn except to us. My church will receive federal aid, in the form of billions of taxpayer dollars, already assured by my friends over there" he gestured to the men from the state department, "to rebuild the city and help the survivors, all of whom now are at our mercy, like always…SLAVES!! ALL OF YOU!!"

He pulled out a key and walked towards a control panel,
"We have allowed too much freedom, it ends tonight." The Seer turned the key.

BOOM! BOOM! BOOM! BOOM! BOOM!
BOOM! Gunshots echoed through the command chamber! Skud looked up and saw a man with slicked back blonde hair in a trench coat, the cop who had been chasing them, Detective Moe Scheffield, standing with his gun up, smoke rising from the barrel. The men at the table fell to the ground, as did The Seer. Skud couldn't believe it, saved by a cop. No shit. The detective ran over to Skud, smoke now rising around him from the missile,

"Detective Moe Scheffield, Pepper-Mountain City PD, you're under arrest."

"Whatever man just get me off of this fucking thing!" Skud said, looking at Moe. 20.. 19.. 18… a robotic woman's voice rang through the chamber, alarms blaring. Skud felt the rocket rumbling as the engines fired, Moe Scheffield jumped back.

"grrrghh… cough…cough…" a grumble came from The Seer, bleeding on the floor, "it's too late…agh..haha-haha…...unnnhhh…." Moe stepped back, looked at Skud and said,

"I'm sorry" looking on in horror, tears in his eyes as the rocket lifted upwards.

Skud felt the pressure on his face and body as the missile gained velocity upwards through the air. He felt the skin on his face start to peel off as the rocket started to curve and gain even more speed. Skud tried to scream but nothing came out, he couldn't, the wind and force were too much. The rocket roared through the sky and Skud could see Pepper-Mountain city. He heard a thud and started to fall out of the sky, the first stage had released, the warhead was on its way. Falling from the clouds, stuck to this hunk of metal, Skud heard his father's drunken words echoed in his head,

"It's a long way down bro, hope you got wings."

"Figures" he thought to himself. Still falling and watching the warhead veer closer and closer to the city, he thought, thought about all of the people in that city, in the world…all of the children, the families…everyone. All of their futures ripped from underneath them. They were the lucky ones, the survivors would now have to live in a world pre-manufactured for them out of hate and malice, without a clue. Willing calves for the slaughter…

Tears filled Skud's eyes as a brilliant white light erupted in the distance,

"Beautiful" he thought when he saw it and then he saw nothing. Blind, in the darkness, he felt warmth on his face and then intense heat searing his flesh, and then… nothing…the dominos had fallen…a shitty end to a shitty life…...

THE END

Stay tuned for the next action-packed graphic novel from Frenetic Creations! "The Reptillian Hunter"

Coming 2026...

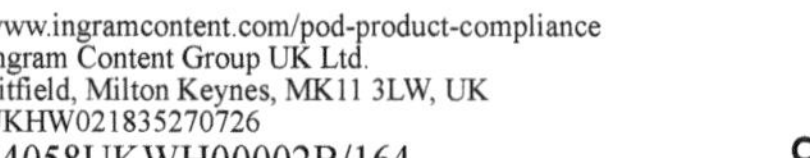
www.ingramcontent.com/pod-product-compliance
Ingram Content Group UK Ltd.
Pitfield, Milton Keynes, MK11 3LW, UK
UKHW021835270726
14058UKWH00002B/164

9 798218 206130